MACDONALD YOUNG BOOKS

The wife was the children's stepmother and she didn't care for them much. Times were very hard and there was hardly a scrap of food in the house. "What will become of us?" sighed the woodcutter one evening. "How will we feed the children?"

"Never mind about them," said the wife. "What about us? I think we should take them into the middle of the forest and leave them there. They'll never find their way back."

"I couldn't do a cruel thing like that," said the woodcutter.

"Then we'll all starve," said the wife and she nagged him so much that at last he gave in.

When they woke up it was dark.
"How will we ever find our way home?"
cried Gretel.

"Wait till moonrise," said her brother.
"Then you'll see."

Sure enough, as soon as the moon rose in the sky it picked out the trail of shining white pebbles that Hansel had so carefully laid. Hand in hand, the whole night long, the children followed the pebbles until at last they were home.

but only went further and deeper into the forest. They wandered all night and all of the next day too, with only a few berries they found on the bushes to eat. When they were too tired to drag themselves any further they fell asleep beneath a tree.

On the third morning they set off again. They were so hungry. "Oh, I could eat a whole house," said Hansel to his sister.

At that moment they saw a snow-white bird sitting on a branch and singing the sweetest song. It flitted from tree to tree so that Hansel and Gretel could follow. At last it landed softly on the roof of a very strange cottage. When the children went close up to it they found that the walls were made of gingerbread, the roof of cakes, and the windows of spun sugar.

"What a feast," said Hansel. "I will eat a
piece of the roof, you try the window."
They had each broken off a piece when a
gentle voice called from inside the cottage.
"Tip-tap, tip-tap, who goes rip-rap?"

The children answered, "Never mind, it's only the wind," and went on eating. Hansel found the roof quite delicious while Gretel thought the window-pane was the sweetest thing she'd ever tasted.

They were still feasting away when a very old woman came out with fiery red eyes. The children were terrified but the old woman spoke to them kindly.

"Hello, little children. What brings you to my cottage? Come in and have something to eat."

Inside the cottage the table was laid with milk and pancakes and honey and apples and

nuts. When Hansel and Gretel had eaten and drunk their fill the old woman showed them to two little beds, so soft that they immediately fell into a heavenly sleep.

Although the old woman seemed so kind, Hansel and Gretel might have guessed from her fiery red eyes that she was really a wicked witch. She had built the bread house in order to tempt little children so that she could kill them, cook them and eat them up! Her fiery red eyes could not see very far, but she had a beast's sense of smell. She had a specially good nose for children.

She gazed at them as they slept, with their rosy cheeks and soft breathing. "What a lovely bite they will make," she cackled.

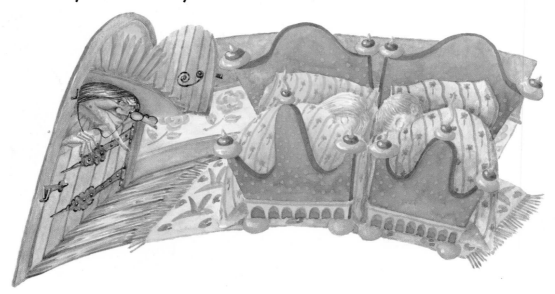

At the crack of dawn she dragged Hansel out of bed and locked him up in a little cage. "Get some water to cook something for your brother," she ordered Gretel, "I intend to fatten him up and eat him!"

Gretel was forced to do as she said. Every day, Hansel got a good meal while all Gretel got was a crab's claw. Every day the witch went to the cage and said, "Put out your finger, dear little boy, so that I can tell whether you are fat enough to eat."

But instead of putting out a finger, Hansel put out an old bone.

When four weeks had passed and Hansel had grown no fatter, the witch finally lost her temper. "Be he fat or be he thin, I'll boil a pot to cook him in!" she cried.

How Gretel wept! And how frightened
Hansel was! But it did no good. "First we'll
bake some bread to go with the boy," said the
witch. "I have heated the oven and kneaded
the dough." She pushed Gretel towards the
oven. "Creep in to make sure it is hot
enough," she said.

Of course, she intended to close the door
of the oven as soon as Gretel was inside and
eat her as well.

Gretel looked at the burning oven and said, "I don't know how to do it, will you show me?"

"Stupid goose!" said the old woman. "Like this!"

They found their father all alone, sitting sadly in a chair. His wife had died and he had not had one happy hour since leaving his children in the forest.

Gretel shook her apron, scattering pearls and precious stones all over the floor, while Hansel emptied his pockets.

Now all their troubles were over and they lived happily ever after.

Other titles available in the Classic Fairy Tales series:

Cinderella
Retold by Adèle Geras   Illustrated by Gwen Tourret

The Ugly Ducking
Retold by Sally Grindley   Illustrated by Bert Kitchen

Beauty and the Beast
Retold by Philippa Pearce   Illustrated by James Mayhew

Little Red Riding Hood
Retold by Sam McBratney   Illustrated by Emma Chichester Clark

Rapunzel
Retold by James Reeves   Illustrated by Sophie Allsopp

Jack and the Beanstalk
Retold by Josephine Poole   Illustrated by Paul Hess

Snow White and the Seven Dwarfs
Retold by Jenny Koralek   Illustrated by Susan Scott

Hansel and Gretel
Retold by Joyce Dunbar   Illustrated by Ian Penney

Thumbelina
Retold by Jenny Nimmo   Illustrated by Phillida Gili

Snow-White and Rose-Red
Retold by Antonia Barber   Illustrated by Gilly Marklew

Sleeping Beauty
Retold by Ann Turnbull   Illustrated by Sophy Williams

Rumpelstiltskin
Retold by Helen Cresswell   Illustrated by John Howe

Goldilocks and the Three Bears
Retold by Penelope Lively   Illustrated by Debi Gliori